PUFFIN BOOKS

MAGIC IN THE AIR

Linda Chapman lives in Leicestershire with her family and two Bernese mountain dogs. When she is not writing she spends her time looking after her two young daughters, horse riding and teaching drama.

Stardust
MAGIC IN THE AIR

Linda Chapman
Illustrated by Angie Thompson

PUFFIN

To Jasmine Ivory – for inspiring Lucy ★

PUFFIN BOOKS

Published by the Penguin Group
Penguin Books Ltd, 80 Strand, London WC2R 0RL, England
Penguin Group (USA) Inc., 375 Hudson Street, New York, New York 10014, USA
Penguin Group (Canada), 90 Eglinton Avenue East, Suite 700, Toronto, Ontario, Canada M4P 2Y3
(a division of Pearson Penguin Canada Inc.)
Penguin Ireland, 25 St Stephen's Green, Dublin 2, Ireland (a division of Penguin Books Ltd)
Penguin Group (Australia), 250 Camberwell Road, Camberwell, Victoria 3124, Australia
(a division of Pearson Australia Group Pty Ltd)
Penguin Books India Pvt Ltd, 11 Community Centre, Panchsheel Park, New Delhi – 110 017, India
Penguin Group (NZ), cnr Airborne and Rosedale Roads, Albany, Auckland 1310, New Zealand
(a division of Pearson New Zealand Ltd)
Penguin Books (South Africa) (Pty) Ltd, 24 Sturdee Avenue, Rosebank, Johannesburg 2196,
South Africa

Penguin Books Ltd, Registered Offices: 80 Strand, London WC2R 0RL, England

www.penguin.com

First published 2005
1

Text copyright © Linda Chapman, 2005
Illustrations copyright © Angie Thompson, 2005
All rights reserved

The moral right of the author and illustrator has been asserted

Set in Monotype Bembo
Made and printed in England by Clays Ltd, St Ives plc

British Library Cataloguing in Publication Data
A CIP catalogue record for this book is available from the British Library

ISBN 0–141–31781–7

The night breeze whispered through the leaves of the nearby trees. Lucy took a deep breath – this was the moment she had been waiting for. The moment when she finally got to try doing her higher stardust magic. Feeling very excited, she tucked her long chestnut-brown hair behind her ears. *Please let me be able to do it*, she thought.

Hearing a rustle she glanced around. A dog fox was padding out of the trees around the edge of the clearing. He gave her a curious look and then trotted on his way, his russet-red fur gleaming in the moonlight. Lucy smiled and watched him go. It was weird to think that just a few months ago she would have been very scared if she had found herself alone in the middle of the woods at midnight. But that was before she'd discovered that she was a stardust spirit. Stardust spirits lived like normal people in the day but at night-time they said the magic words that turned them into their stardust form and they flew to the woods to watch over plants and animals, looking out for any disturbances in nature and putting right any problems caused by thoughtless

humans. Lucy loved everything about
being a stardust spirit. She loved meeting
up with her friends in the woods each
night, she loved being able to fly, she loved
being able to get close to wild animals but
most of all she loved being able to do
magic!

There were four types of stardust spirit.
Being a summer stardust spirit, Lucy could
use magic to heat things up and start fires.
She could also conjure an invisible shield
that could protect anyone or anything
from harm, but that was higher magic – a
very difficult type of magic and Lucy had
only just started learning how to do it.
Rebecca, the adult summer spirit who was
teaching her how to use her higher
powers, had said that she could have her
first go at conjuring a shield that very

night. Lucy had been unable to think
about anything else all day.

Looking around the clearing, she hoped
Rebecca would arrive soon. The stars
overhead were glittering brightly and the
air felt as if it was tingling with magic.
Lucy's eyes fell on a dead branch lying on
the grass. *I could always practise my normal
summer magic while I'm waiting,* she thought
to herself. *I could just start a small fire.*

Excitement flared through her. She knew she had to be careful about starting a fire in the woods but doing magic was so much fun she just couldn't resist it.

It'll be fine, she decided. *Nothing will go wrong.* She pointed at the branch and whispered, 'Fire be with me!'

Power exploded up through her arms and out through her fingertips. The branch burst into flame.

For a moment, Lucy was almost taken aback by how easy it had been but she knew she had to keep concentrating on the fire. It could so easily get out of control. Focusing on the flames, Lucy forced the fire down with her mind. It got smaller and smaller and finally died away, leaving just a blackened scar of burnt wood on the forest floor.

'Well done.'

Lucy swung around. Rebecca was watching her from the edge of the clearing, her beautiful golden dress glinting in the starlight. 'You controlled that fire very well,' she said.

Lucy felt a glow of pride. 'Thanks.'

Rebecca walked over. 'It's unusual for a stardust spirit as young as you to be able to start fires, Lucy. Most can only warm things up. I hope you find doing your higher magic just as easy. Are you ready to have a try at conjuring a shield?'

'Yes please!' Lucy said eagerly.

'Do you remember what you have to do?' Rebecca asked.

'I have to shut my eyes and imagine the exact pattern of stars that make out the shape of a lion in the night sky,' Lucy told her. 'It's called the constellation of Leo.'

Rebecca nodded. 'And why do you have to see Leo?'

'Because Regulus, the royal summer star, is part of Leo. My magic comes from Regulus because I'm a summer stardust spirit like you,' Lucy replied promptly.

'Good girl.' Rebecca looked pleased. She picked up a leaf from the ground. 'Now, imagine Leo in your mind. If you do it well, you should feel power flowing into you from Regulus. Say, "Shield be with me," open your eyes and focus on this leaf. If your magic works you should be able to conjure a magic shield that will stop me from harming it. Concentrate now. You have to be able to see every single star of Leo in your mind or the magic won't work.'

Lucy shut her eyes and pictured the constellation. She started with the six stars rather like a question mark that marked out Leo's head, mane and shoulder.

Her arms tingled. *It's happening,* she thought excitedly as she felt the flow of magic power. She wondered if her friends were managing to use their higher magic too. *I bet Allegra will be doing really well,* she decided. *Allegra's always so good at everything . . .*

'Concentrate, Lucy.' Rebecca's soft voice interrupted her thoughts.

With a start, Lucy realized that the tingling feeling had stopped.

'You must push everything else out of your mind,' Rebecca instructed. 'Just focus on Leo.'

Lucy nodded and tried again. One by

one the stars popped into her mind. Leo's neck, mane, front leg, hindquarters, tail . . .

Magic surged through her, swift and strong. Lucy gasped at the power of it.

'Shield be with me!' she cried, pointing at the leaf in Rebecca's hand.

Rebecca tried to crumple the leaf up into a ball but as soon as she released it, it sprang back into shape.

Lucy's blood felt as if it was burning but she didn't care. Her body seemed to be glowing with power. She felt strong, unstoppable – as if she could do anything she wanted.

Rebecca tried to tear the leaf but it simply bent and flexed under her fingers. Putting it on the ground, she stamped on it but the leaf remained unharmed.

A smile broke out on Rebecca's face.

'That's very good, Lucy. Now let the power go.'

Lucy hesitated. The power was beating through her. She didn't want to let it go. She wanted to hold on to it. To let it grow, get *stronger* . . .

'Lucy?' Rebecca said. A frown suddenly creased her forehead. 'Lucy,' she commanded, 'let the power go!'

With a sigh, Lucy let the image of the constellation fade from her mind. The tingling stopped. Lucy blinked. She felt dizzy, light-headed, like she was going to giggle. 'Oh wow!' she exclaimed, her greeny-grey eyes shining. 'That . . . that was fantastic!'

'You cast an extremely protective shield.' There was a strange note in Rebecca's voice; she sounded almost concerned. 'To

be able to do that your first time is
extremely rare indeed.'

'It felt brilliant!' Lucy enthused.

'You're going to be a very powerful
spirit one day, Lucy,' Rebecca said slowly.

Lucy grinned at her. She *wanted* to be
powerful. She wanted to be the most
powerful stardust spirit there had ever
been. Doing magic was amazing! 'Can I
have another go?'

To her disappointment, Rebecca shook
her head. 'Another night. Why don't you
go and wait for your friends to finish their
lessons? I'm sure they won't be long.'

Lucy nodded and, saying goodbye to
Rebecca, she flew to the clearing where
her best friend, Allegra, was practising with
her mum, Xanthe. Allegra was the only
one of Lucy's friends who had a parent

who was a stardust spirit. It had been
Allegra and Xanthe who had explained
about the stardust world to Lucy, the day
they had moved into the cottage next
door to Lucy's.

Now that she didn't have to concentrate
on her higher magic, Lucy began to
wonder again how Allegra was getting on
practising her powers. She knew Allegra
would be doing a different magic to her
because Allegra was an autumn spirit.
There were four types of stardust spirit –
spring, summer, autumn and winter – and
each had different magical powers. Being
an autumn spirit, Allegra had the power to
read the worries in people's hearts. The
most powerful autumn spirits could even
read people's thoughts and discover exactly
what they were thinking.

★

To Lucy's surprise, Allegra was looking mutinous. 'It's boring!' she was saying to Xanthe. 'I don't want to concentrate on imagining Scorpio.'

'But, Allegra, you have to concentrate if you're going to use your higher powers,' Xanthe said.

But Allegra had spotted Lucy. 'Can we stop now, Xanthe?' She always called her mum by her real name, something Lucy had found weird at first. However, now she was very used to it.

'All right.' Xanthe sighed. 'Off you go.'

Allegra flew up into the sky and joined Lucy. 'I'm glad that's over. I was getting *so* bored!'

'Bored?' Lucy said, looking at her best friend in surprise. 'It was cool. I really enjoyed using my powers.'

'What? Shutting your eyes and picturing a constellation?' Allegra said. She spun on the spot and her shoulder-length blonde curls flew out in a halo around her. 'I'd far rather be flying. Come on, let's play tag.' She touched Lucy's arm. 'You're on!'

Tag was great fun, especially when you could fly! Lucy raced towards Allegra.

Allegra ducked away from her outstretched hand. 'So did *you* do your magic?' she shouted as she swooped away.

'Yes,' Lucy gasped, flying after her. 'I made this magic shield and protected a leaf. It was an amazing feeling. So didn't you manage to do yours?'

'No,' Allegra replied. 'But I bet Ella and Faye haven't managed either.'

She slowed up and Lucy saw her opportunity. 'Got you! You're on!'

As she dived away from Allegra, Lucy saw their other two friends, Faye and Ella, flying into the clearing. 'Hi!' she called, flying over.

'Wasn't that brilliant?' Ella exclaimed, her brown eyes alight, her black ponytail bouncing on her shoulders.

'Did you use your powers?' Lucy asked excitedly.

'Yes, I disguised a log to look like a mound of grass.' Being a spring spirit, Ella had the power to conjure magic disguises.

'And I managed to heal a graze on Samantha's arm,' Faye said. She was smaller than Ella with short blonde hair that framed her heart-shaped face. She was a winter spirit and had the power to heal. 'Did you two manage to use your powers too?'

'I did,' Lucy replied. 'But Allegra didn't.'

'You didn't?' Ella looked at Allegra in surprise.

'No.' Allegra shrugged unconcernedly. 'But it was only because I got bored. Xanthe just kept making me think about the constellation over and over again. I'll do my magic tomorrow, no problem.'

Ella looked serious. 'Actually, it isn't that easy, Allegra. I had to try nine times before I could use my magic. It was really hard and you haven't got an easy constellation to remember. Scorpio's got loads of stars in it.'

'But I'm sure you'll manage to do it,' Faye put in quickly as Allegra began to frown. 'You're really good at doing magic, Allegra.'

Allegra's frown faded. 'Yes, I'll be fine,'

she said confidently. Her blue eyes darted around. 'What shall we do now? How about a race to that big beech tree near the hazel grove?'

'We should really go and see what jobs need doing,' Ella said responsibly. Every night the older stardust spirits gave the four of them tasks to do around the woods. Being nine years old, Lucy and her friends were the youngest spirits in the woods.

'We can ask later,' Allegra said. 'Let's have a race now.'

'We really should –' Ella began.

'Bet I can get there first!' Allegra interrupted and she raced off.

Lucy hesitated for a moment and then plunged after her.

Together they flew through the trees.

The wind whipped against Lucy's cheeks
as she forced the air behind her with her
mind. She was going to get there first! The
majestic beech tree loomed up in the
distance. Lucy sped towards it and reached
out her hand. But Allegra surged ahead
and tagged it first.

'Beat you!' she gasped.

'Only just!' Lucy panted. They grinned
at each other.

Allegra looked around. 'Where are Ella
and Faye?'

As she spoke, Ella and Faye came flying
towards them. Ella was looking cross. Faye
put on a burst of speed and reached the
tree trunk just before her.

'First, second, third,' Allegra said,
pointing to herself, then Lucy, then Faye.
'And last,' she grinned, pointing to Ella.

Ella frowned. 'You had a head start. And anyway, I *do* think we should have gone to find your mum and asked what she wanted us to do.'

Allegra looked at her teasingly. 'You're just in a mood cos you didn't win.'

'I'm not,' Ella said crossly.

'You are.'

Lucy sighed. Allegra was obviously in one of her annoying moods. It was bound to lead to an argument with Ella, who hated being teased. She tried to distract them. 'What should we do now?'

Ella looked stubborn. 'I think we should go back,' she said, folding her arms.

'Boring!' Allegra declared.

'Why don't we go and check on the old crow's nest in the branches?' Faye suggested quickly. 'We could see if there are any birds nesting in it.'

Ella ignored her. 'I am *not* boring!' she said to Allegra. 'You *know* we're supposed to ask what needs doing.'

'Come on, you two,' Lucy urged, flying between them. 'It's a really good idea of Faye's. Let's look for eggs and we can go back and see Xanthe later.'

'Yes, come on!' Faye said, flying up into the green canopy of leaves.

But Ella continued to glare at Allegra. 'You think you're so cool, don't you, Allegra? But you couldn't even do your higher magic tonight.'

'I could!' Allegra replied. 'I just didn't feel like it.'

'Yeah, right!' Ella frowned.

'Stop it, you two!' Lucy said in

frustration. 'You're being –'

She was interrupted by Faye flying down from the tree. 'Hey!' Faye gasped. 'You've got to come and see this nest. There's a big bird with a hooked beak. It looks like it's some sort of bird of prey.'

'Really?' said Allegra.

'Birds of prey are really rare!' Ella exclaimed. 'They're endangered and as stardust spirits we're supposed to protect them.'

The argument was immediately forgotten.

'What type of bird of prey?' Allegra asked eagerly. 'Is it a kestrel or a hawk or something else?'

'I don't know,' Faye answered. 'It's sort of grey and white and there are two eggs in the nest. Come and see!'

Two

The four girls flew up into the branches of the beech tree. There was an old crow's nest in the fork of the tree. It was made out of dried twigs but now they were closer they could see that fresh green branches had been recently added.

'Look!' Lucy whispered, as she saw a bird sitting on the nest. It was a large bird with a small head and a heavy-set body

covered in browny-grey feathers. Its dark
eyes were half closed and its slender
curved beak was resting on its chest.

'It's a honey buzzard!' Allegra hissed.
'They're really rare!' Allegra knew more
about the animals and birds in the forest
than any of them. 'They spend the winter
in Africa and then come here in the
summer to breed. I bet there's another one
here somewhere. They mate for life.'

'There!' Ella whispered suddenly. She
pointed through the leaves. On a nearby
branch was another honey buzzard, slightly
smaller than the first. It was watching them
with unblinking dark eyes. Like all the other
animals and birds in the forest, it seemed to
understand that because the girls were
stardust spirits, they were no threat and
there was no need to be frightened of them.

'That must be the mother bird,' Lucy said. 'It's smaller.'

Allegra shook her head. 'With birds of prey, the male bird is usually smaller so that's probably the father.' She looked at Faye. 'Did you say you saw some eggs?'

'Yes, two,' Faye answered. 'They were white with purply-red blotches.'

'We should go and tell Xanthe,' Allegra said. 'She'll want to know about them so that she can organize for this pair to be protected. It would be awful if something happened to their eggs.'

They flew back to the clearing. Xanthe was delighted to hear the news.

'A pair of honey buzzards! That's wonderful!' she exclaimed, her face lighting up. 'There're only about sixty of

them in the whole country at the
moment. We'll have to protect their
eggs. There are lots of people who
would be interested in collecting them
and selling them.'

'Selling them?' Ella echoed.

'Yes,' Xanthe replied. 'There's a big
market in rare birds' eggs at the moment.
They get sold over the Internet. So you
mustn't tell anyone who isn't a stardust
spirit about the nest. We'll try to keep it
safe until the chicks hatch.'

'When will that be?' Faye asked.

'Very soon, I'd imagine,' Xanthe
answered. 'Honey buzzard eggs have
usually hatched out so this may well be a
second clutch. If these eggs are lost then
the adults won't lay any more this year.'
She ran a hand through her blonde hair.

'I'll have to sort out some sort of rota with the other spirits so that we can keep an eye on the nest.'

'We'll help, won't we?' Lucy said, looking round at the others. They all nodded eagerly.

'We could watch over the nest every night until the chicks hatch out,' Ella said.

'That would be great,' Xanthe replied. 'Like I say, it really shouldn't be too long and then the danger from human egg collectors will be over. Just remember, though,' she warned, 'you're only there to watch out for danger. If people do come you mustn't get involved. Come here and tell me or one of the other adults.' She looked round at them all firmly. 'Remember, you're not experienced enough to use your magic around people.

They might see you and that would be disastrous. The stardust world *must* be kept secret. Do you understand?'

They all nodded.

'Good.' Xanthe smiled. 'Now, why don't you fly back to that tree and keep watch?'

'OK,' Lucy and her friends chorused.

They flew back to the beech tree and landed on its sturdy lower branches.

'Isn't this cool?' Ella said as they all sat down. 'Out of sixty honey buzzards in the country, we're looking after two of them!'

Lucy nodded. 'We'll make sure the chicks hatch out safely.'

Faye shivered. 'I hope egg collectors don't come.'

'Well, if they do, we just go and get help,' Ella said practically.

'Or we sort them out ourselves,' Allegra

put in.

Ella frowned. 'We're not allowed. You heard what your mum said.'

'So?' Allegra grinned mischievously. 'Can you imagine how much fun it would be to try out our magic on people?'

Ella looked shocked. 'It would be wrong.'

Allegra sighed. '*Ella!*'

'You know what, we should think of some names for the birds,' Lucy said quickly. She didn't want Ella and Allegra to start arguing again. 'What shall we call them?'

'Something beginning with B,' Faye said. 'Because they're buzzards.'

'How about Bob for the male bird?' Lucy suggested.

'Yeah!' Allegra exclaimed. 'And then the

female can be Wendy.'

Ella frowned. 'Wendy? Wendy doesn't start with a B.'

Lucy grinned at Allegra. She had a feeling she knew what Allegra was thinking. 'No, but remember when we were younger? Wendy goes with Bob – Bob the builder.'

'Oh,' Ella said, looking a bit confused.

Faye giggled. 'I like Bob and Wendy. Let's call them that!'

'Agreed,' Allegra declared. 'Now what we should think about is how we're going to use our magic to protect the eggs.'

As they made plans about how they could best protect the birds, the evening flew by. Soon Ella's constellation – Taurus – was rising in the sky and it was time to fly home.

They arranged to meet at the beech tree
the next night and then set off. As Lucy
flew through the sky with Allegra, she
scanned the stars. She could see the Great
Bear and Little Bear and Pegasus flying
through the sky. It was wonderful being
able to make out their patterns, to know
their names. *This is my world*, she thought
happily. When she was flying like this it
was hard to imagine that in just a few
hours' time she would be waking up in
her bedroom, about to continue with her
ordinary nine-year-old life.

The sun streamed through Lucy's open
window, falling on her face and waking
her up. As she blinked her eyes open, she
remembered the night before. The honey
buzzards! She pictured the browny-grey

bird sitting on her nest and smiled.

Jumping out of bed, she went downstairs. Her dad was in the kitchen. Lucy wished she could tell him about the amazing birds of prey and their nest. He loved wildlife and often told Lucy about the times he had spent in the woods when he was younger. He had seen badgers, fox cubs, rabbits. He had even had a dormouse as a pet once. Lucy had an idea. She knew she couldn't tell her dad about the honey buzzards nesting in the woods, but maybe she could ask him if he had ever seen any of the birds himself.

'Dad,' Lucy asked, 'have you ever seen a honey buzzard?'

'A honey buzzard,' her dad echoed. 'Yes, actually I have. A pair nested in the woods for a while when I was about ten. They

33

weren't quite so rare then as they are now but they were still pretty unusual.' He looked at her curiously. 'Why?'

'Oh I just saw something about them on telly,' Lucy said quickly. 'They look amazing.'

'They are,' her dad commented, 'particularly when they fly. I've got a book in the lounge about birds of prey and that's got some pictures of honey buzzards flying. Do you want me to find it for you?'

'Yes please,' Lucy replied eagerly.

She followed him through to the lounge. Rachel, her middle sister, was sitting on the sofa in her riding clothes. She was watching television.

'Here's the book,' Mr Evans said, going to the bookcase and taking out a large book. 'Now let's see if we can find honey

34

buzzards.' He flicked through the pages. 'Here we are. I thought there were some good pictures.'

Lucy took the book. On one of the pages there was a photograph of a bird just like the two she had seen the night before. It stared out of the book haughtily.

'I bet that's a female,' Lucy said, seeing how big and solid it looked.

Her dad nodded. 'I think you're right. It's too big to be a male. Birds of prey are quite unusual because –'

'– the female is usually bigger than the male,' Lucy finished for him.

Her dad looked impressed. 'That's right. Well done, Lucy.'

Rachel looked over her shoulder. 'What are you doing?'

'Lucy wanted to see some pictures of a

rare type of bird called a honey buzzard,' their dad said.

Rachel looked astonished. 'Why?'

Lucy shrugged. 'Because I'm interested.' She knew Rachel wouldn't understand. Rachel wasn't into wildlife. In fact, she never took anything seriously.

Rachel grinned. 'You know, you get more geeky every day!'

'I don't!' Lucy protested.

'Next you'll be taking up a really dorky hobby like birdwatching!' Rachel teased.

Mr Evans frowned. 'That's enough, Rachel. It would be good to see you doing something constructive like reading a wildlife book instead of watching rubbish on television.' The phone rang and he went to answer it. As he left the lounge, Hope, Lucy and Rachel's older sister, walked in.

'Come on, Rach. We should go to the stables. If we don't leave in the next five minutes, we'll be late.'

'All right, stop stressing,' Rachel said, standing up. She grinned at Lucy. 'See you later, Geek-brain.'

Lucy glared at her. Rachel could be *really* annoying at times!

As the door shut behind her sisters, Lucy sat down on the sofa. She looked back at the pages on honey buzzards. There were two pictures of birds soaring over the countryside, their wings outstretched.

Lucy smiled to herself and felt her irritation with Rachel fading from her mind. She knew what flying felt like. She had a secret life her annoying sister would never even dream of.

She touched the picture. 'I'll protect you,' she whispered, thinking about the two buzzards in the woods. 'Me, Allegra, Ella and Faye. We all will!'

Three

'I believe in stardust,' Lucy breathed as she stood by her open window, the starlight falling on her arms and face. 'I believe in stardust. I believe in stardust!'

As she spoke the final words, she felt a warmth rush through her body and then she seemed to be melting, dissolving . . .

The next moment, she was flying out of the window and into the night sky. Her pyjamas had turned into her golden stardust dress. The four different types of stardust spirit each wore different colour clothes. Autumn spirits like Allegra wore silver, winter spirits like Faye wore blue and spring spirits like Ella wore green. Lucy loved being a summer spirit; her dress glittered and shone like the rays of the sun. She twirled in the air, enjoying the feel of the wind on her face, and then she swooped over the garden fence.

Allegra was waiting. The two of them headed across the fields towards the woods.

'Are we going straight to the buzzards?' Lucy asked.

Allegra nodded. 'I told Xanthe we'd go and check on them first thing. She said not to worry about our other jobs for a while – at least not until the eggs hatch.

Keeping them safe is really important.'

As they flew through the sky, Lucy could see a bright star shining in the distance. It was so much brighter than any of the other stars that she thought it must be one of the Royal Stars – the four brightest stars in the sky that gave all stardust spirits their magic powers. 'Is that Antares?' she asked.

Allegra followed her gaze and nodded. Antares was the star of the autumn spirits.

Lucy studied it. 'So how does it fit into the Scorpion constellation?'

'Well, you can't see all of the Scorpion at the moment,' Allegra explained. 'You can just see the head and the first part of the body. Do you see those three stars that sort of go in a line?' Lucy nodded. 'Well, they're the Scorpion's head and Antares

42

and the stars next to it are the first bits of
its body. There are another ten stars that
you can't see at the moment. When the
constellation's higher in the sky you can
see it more easily.'

Lucy looked at her curiously. 'You know
what it looks like really well. How come
you couldn't picture it yesterday to do
your higher magic?'

Allegra shrugged. 'I just got bored. I *can*
picture it; I just don't like *having* to.'

Lucy nodded. Knowing Allegra, it made
sense. Allegra hated being made to do
things. 'Will you try again tonight?' she
asked. 'It would be cool if you could use
your higher powers too.'

'I guess.' Allegra sounded unconcerned.
'I'll just have to see if I feel like it.' She
flew to Lucy and touched her arm. 'Tag!

You're on!'

Before Lucy could say anything Allegra was racing away through the trees.

Lucy followed her swiftly and they continued to play tag until they arrived at the buzzards' tree.

Ella and Faye were already there.

'Hi!' Lucy panted. Suddenly she noticed that Ella and Faye were both looking worried. Her heart lurched. 'What's the matter?' she said quickly. 'Has anything happened to the birds?'

'No, it's OK,' Faye replied. 'They're fine. It's just that a clearing nearby has been disturbed.'

'Disturbed? What do you mean?' Allegra demanded.

'There's litter and the remains of a fire,' Ella replied. 'It looks like a group of people

44

have been there. The birds seem OK, but the people might have seen them flying about.'

Lucy and Allegra exchanged worried glances.

'Come and see,' Ella said.

Lucy and Allegra followed her and Faye through the trees until they came to a clearing at the end of one of the forest tracks. The grass had been trampled and there was a charred circle where a fire had been lit. Ten empty cans and some crisp packets littered the ground.

'It's a bit of a mess,' Lucy said. 'We should clear it up.'

'Yeah, and some of that hornbeam needs regrowing,' Allegra added, pointing to where some young hornbeam trees had been flattened and a few branches torn off for the fire.

Faye looked worried. 'What if the people saw the birds?'

'They probably wouldn't have known they were rare birds,' Allegra told her. 'It looks like it was just a group of teenagers. You often get teenagers hanging out in the woods in the summer.'

'Maybe we should go and tell your mum,' Ella said anxiously.

'We'll tell her later. Let's tidy up now,' Allegra replied.

They started to pick the litter up. There was a forest car park five minutes away. They flew there with the cans and crisp packets and then Ella used her magic powers to regrow the hornbeam. Being a spring spirit she could make things grow; autumn spirits could conjure wind and winter spirits could make it rain or snow.

'That looks much better,' Allegra declared, glancing approvingly around at the clearing. 'Now what shall we do?'

'Let's try using our higher magic,' Ella suggested eagerly. 'I spent all morning looking at pictures of my constellation on the Internet. I kept shutting my eyes and then trying to draw the constellation on paper. I didn't stop until I could position all the stars perfectly the second I tried. I really want to have a go at disguising something and see if it's easier than it was last night.'

'OK,' Lucy said to her. 'Go on then.'

Ella looked around. 'I'll disguise that bramble bush over there. Watch.' She shut her eyes and a look of intense concentration furrowed her forehead. 'Disguise be with me,' she whispered and then, opening her eyes, she pointed at the bush.

For a moment, the air around the bush seemed to flicker and then suddenly the bush wasn't there any more. At least it was, but it now looked like a rhododendron, the tiny unripe berries replaced by big pink flowers and the dull green foliage turned into big shiny leaves.

'That's brilliant!' Faye exclaimed.

'Yeah, really cool, Ella!' Allegra said.

Lucy could hardly believe her eyes. She walked over to the rhododendron. The air around it still seemed to shimmer slightly. She reached out curiously. Was it really a rhododendron? 'Ow!' she gasped, pulling her hand away as an unseen bramble thorn pricked her.

'It's not really a rhododendron, Luce,' Ella said. 'It just looks like one. It's an illusion.' She waved her hands. 'Disguise be

gone!' she commanded.

Lucy blinked. The rhododendron was once more just a bramble bush. She turned to Ella. 'That was amazing. You're brilliant at using your higher powers.'

Ella blushed, looking embarrassed but pleased by the praise.

'I'm going to have a go next,' Allegra declared. She grinned at them all. 'Watch out, everyone, I'm going to read your thoughts.'

'You won't really be able to do that, will you?' Faye said nervously. 'I thought it was only really powerful adult stardust spirits who could read thoughts. You won't really be able to see what we're thinking, will you, Allegra?'

Allegra smiled teasingly. 'You never know.'

'Don't worry, Faye,' Ella said quickly. 'She'll just get an idea of what's in our hearts – an idea of what we might be afraid of or looking forward to. Allegra's not powerful enough to read our thoughts properly. She's not going to be able to see exactly what we're thinking.'

'Bet I will,' Allegra said confidently. 'Watch out, I'm going to see all the secrets in your mind, Faye,' she teased.

Faye looked alarmed.

Lucy grinned at Allegra. 'Just get on

with it.'

Allegra shut her eyes and frowned in concentration. She held out her hands. 'Thoughts!' she said dramatically. 'Be with me!'

She opened her eyes and looked at Faye for a few seconds with a slightly puzzled frown.

Her eyes suddenly widened. 'That's it! Faye, you're worried about the birds. You think the people who were here might be egg thieves and . . . and . . . you're worried about someone's birthday.'

'My mum's!' Faye said, looking shocked. 'It's only two days away and I haven't got her a present yet.'

Lucy stared at Allegra in astonishment. 'Did you really see that? You're not just making it up?'

'I really saw it,' Allegra exclaimed. 'I felt magic flow into me and then these pictures came into my mind. As I thought about them I worked out what Faye was worried about. I saw the buzzards and then a group of suspicious-looking people peering through binoculars. That made me realize that Faye is worried about the birds and then I saw a picture of Faye's mum with a birthday cake and Faye holding her hands out with no present.'

'Wow,' Faye breathed. 'That's amazing, Allegra.'

'Yeah,' Ella said, nodding. 'So could you see anything else?'

'No, and the two pictures I did see were quite blurry and difficult to make out. It felt like I could only see them because they were right at the top of Faye's mind –

they're what she's thinking about quite strongly at the moment,' Allegra replied. 'However, I did get the feeling that if I was more powerful I could have looked deeper. Maybe seen secrets and things like that. But I'm sure you'd have to be a really powerful spirit to read thoughts that well.'

'Wow!' Faye said again, looking at Allegra with real respect. 'Your magic's cool!'

'It's not just my magic,' Allegra pointed out. 'Everyone's is. You can heal things, Lucy can protect things and Ella can disguise things. It's amazing. We're all doing this really strong magic.'

The four girls exchanged looks.

'It's like we're becoming proper powerful stardust spirits!' Lucy said, feeling slightly awestruck.

Allegra shot into the sky and pirouetted. 'We can all use our higher powers!' She swooped down and grabbed Ella's hands. Pulling her up into the sky, she spun around with her, laughing with excitement. 'Isn't it brilliant?'

'Brilliant!' Ella gasped, her long dark hair flying around her shoulders.

Lucy grabbed Faye's hands and pulled her up into the sky to join in. 'We're proper stardust spirits!'

Allegra caught her eye and grinned. 'And just think how much fun we can have now!'

Four

'Mum, I'm going to Allegra's,' Lucy said, going into the kitchen the following afternoon. Her mum was making a cake and Rachel was sitting at the table flicking through a pony magazine.

'Have you everything you need?' Mrs Evans said.

'Yep,' Lucy replied. 'Toothbrush, pyjamas, clothes for tomorrow.'

Xanthe had invited her to stay that night. It was really so Lucy and Allegra could go to the woods as soon as night fell instead of Lucy having to wait for her parents to go to bed but, of course, Lucy hadn't told her mum that!

Mrs Evans smiled at her. 'You spend so much time next door at the moment, Lucy, I don't know why you don't just move in there.'

'Can I?' Lucy said, her eyes teasing.

'Go on, say yes, Mum! Please!' Rachel said. 'It would be cool. I could have her room. It's bigger than mine.' Lucy tried to give her a withering look but Rachel just grinned. 'So what are you going to do tonight? I know! I bet you're going to play fairies. What's your name? Fairy Primrose, isn't it?'

'You know, I don't play fairies any more,' Lucy said crossly. When she had been little she had often pretended to be a fairy called Primrose. It was something Rachel never let her forget.

'Has Allegra got a fairy name too? Do you pretend to fly?' Rachel flapped her arms mockingly. 'Come on, let's fly to our little fairy home,' she said in a mocking babyish voice.

'*Mum!*' Lucy appealed.

Mrs Evans sighed in exasperation. 'Rachel, why do you always have to wind Lucy up?'

Rachel grinned. 'Because it's fun.'

Mrs Evans turned to Lucy. 'Go on, off you go. I'll see you tomorrow morning and have a nice time.'

Lucy quickly kissed her mum and left.

Arghhh! Rachel could be so irritating at times. Sometimes she really *did* feel like moving in next door!

As soon as the sun set that evening, Lucy and Allegra flew to the woods.

'Do you think the buzzard eggs will have hatched?' Lucy asked as they swooped through the trees.

'I hope so,' Allegra answered. 'I can't wait to see the chicks.'

Lucy caught a glimpse of two figures just ahead of them. 'Look, it's Ella and Faye!' She and Allegra sped up.

'Hi!' Lucy called out. 'You're here early.'

'I just kept thinking about the people who had been nearby and wondering if they had seen the birds and come back,' Ella said. 'I wanted to come as early as

we could.'

'You worry too much,' Allegra told her. 'You know Xanthe said it was probably just teenagers when we told her about it last night. She said not to worry and –'

'Sssh!' Faye interrupted, grabbing Allegra's arm. 'There're people down there! Listen!'

They all stopped in mid air. Faye was right. The sound of voices and music playing was carrying through the quiet night air. The sounds were coming from the clearing where the litter had been the day before.

'Quick!' Lucy hissed. 'We'd better camouflage ourselves. We mustn't be seen!'

'Camouflagus!' they all whispered and their outlines merged into the background of the starry sky. It was a type of disguising magic that all stardust spirits could do.

'What do we do now?' Faye said in alarm.

'Go round to the tree another way,' Ella replied.

'No,' Allegra said quickly. 'I think we should go and see who these people are and what they're doing.'

Ella frowned. 'But we're not supposed to go near people.'

'We're only going to see what they're up to,' Allegra told her. 'We won't be seen by them.'

'Allegra's right,' Lucy said. 'We should go and check out what they're doing.'

'I don't know,' Ella said reluctantly. 'I suppose it might be OK so long as we don't go too close.'

Lucy nodded. 'Let's go but make sure

you keep your camouflage up.'

To stay camouflaged stardust spirits had
to keep a small part of their mind on the
spell at all times, drawing down magic
from the stars and using it to make
themselves blend in with the background.
Concentrating on keeping disguised,
Lucy flew towards the people, her heart
beating fast.

As she neared the group she felt Ella and
Faye slow down uncertainly.

Lucy glanced around. She could just

make out their outlines against the starry sky but only because she was looking for them. 'Come on!' she urged.

Ella started to shake her head.

Lucy gave up and turned and carried on with Allegra. Five teenagers were sitting around the remains of a fire – three boys and two girls. They had torches and around them were scattered empty drinks cans. Lucy felt a wave of relief. They didn't look like they were egg collectors. Two boys were arm-wrestling while the other boy was telling a ghost story to the girls, who were giggling and pretending to be scared.

'And then there was a tapping on the floor and a voice said –'

'Don't, Mark!' one of the girls squealed. 'I don't want to hear any more!'

The boy called Mark grinned. 'But this is the best bit, isn't it, Dave?' he said to his friend, a tall lanky boy, who was mid-arm wrestle with his friend.

Lucy watched the tall boy look round and grin. It was strange being able to fly near them and not be seen – strange but fun. She flew back to Ella and Faye. 'It's OK,' she whispered. 'It's just teenagers, like we thought.'

Allegra flew up beside her.

Ella looked worried. 'I'm sure the buzzards won't like all this noise near their nest. What are we going to do?'

'Well, we could always make them leave,' Allegra said slowly.

'What do you mean?' Lucy asked her curiously.

'We could make strange noises and

frighten them off.'

'We can't!' Ella exclaimed. 'We're not allowed to go near people.'

'How about it, Luce?' Allegra demanded.

Lucy hesitated. She knew they shouldn't go but it was a tempting idea. Could they really frighten the teenagers away?

'Come on!' Allegra urged. 'We can pretend to be ghosts and fly about making strange noises. It'll be fun!'

Her daring was infectious.

'OK!' Lucy agreed impulsively.

'Lucy!' Ella exclaimed. She looked at Allegra. 'It's a stupid idea. There's no way I'm going to do it.'

Allegra shrugged. 'OK.' She turned to Faye. 'How about you, Faye?'

'I . . . I . . .' Faye stammered.

'Faye won't do it,' Ella said.

'You're not scared, are you, Faye?' Allegra challenged.

'No,' Faye muttered.

'Well, come on!' Allegra urged.

Faye gulped. 'All right.'

'Faye!' Ella exclaimed furiously.

Allegra turned her back on her. 'OK, how are we going to organize this?'

Excitement surged through Lucy. 'I know,' Lucy said. 'You go around to the north, Faye to the south and I'll go to the east. Once we're all in position make the sound of an owl hooting – and then we can all make scary noises!'

Leaving Ella staring furiously after them, Lucy, Allegra and Faye headed back to the clearing. Dave and his friend had stopped arm-wrestling and had joined the others.

'These woods are really spooky,' one of

the girls was saying.

'You think everything's spooky, Julie,' Mark said.

'Whoooo,' Dave teased.

Julie hit him on the arm. 'Stop it!'

'OK,' Lucy whispered to Allegra and Faye as they stayed in the shadow of a tree and let their camouflage drop slightly so they could just see each other against the stars. 'Let's spread out. Hoot once when you're ready.'

'See you later!' Allegra said, darting off.

'What if something goes wrong?' Faye said, hesitating.

'It won't,' Lucy reassured her although her heart was beating fast. She heard a hoot from the north. 'That's Allegra. Go on, Faye. You have to go!'

'I don't want to,' Faye replied, sounding

scared.

'OK, stay here with me,' Lucy told her. She hooted back twice. Almost immediately a strange, moaning, ghostly noise came from Allegra's direction. The teenagers jumped about a foot in the air.

'What's that?' Julie gasped.

'I . . . I don't know,' one of her friends stammered.

Seeing the alarm on their faces, Lucy felt a desperate urge to laugh. She opened her mouth. 'Whooooo,' she called.

The girls both squealed. 'It's a ghost!' Julie exclaimed.

'Don't be daft,' Dave said.

'Maybe it's one of those birds,' the other girl suggested. 'You know, those big brown-and-white ones we saw flying around yesterday.'

Lucy froze. So the teenagers *had* seen the honey buzzards. She hoped they didn't realize how rare the birds were. But Dave's next words made her blood run cold.

'They're really rare those birds,' he said. 'Mark looked them up on the Internet. The eggs are really valuable. It said people pay loads of money for them and . . .'

Mark kicked him.

'Ow!' Dave exclaimed. 'What did you do that for?' But before Mark could answer Julie screamed and pointed just to the right of Lucy.

Lucy swung round.

Faye was visible!

'It's a person!' Julie screamed. 'It's a person in the sky!'

Five

In an instant, Faye disappeared again, merging into the background of the stars.

'Faye!' Lucy whispered in horror. 'They saw you!'

'What do you mean, there's a person?' Mark demanded, looking around wildly. 'There's nothing there.'

'There was. It was in the sky!' Julie could hardly get the words out. 'It was a girl. In a blue dress!'

She looked so terrified that even the boys started to look nervous.

'I'm getting out of here!' Dave's friend muttered.

'Yeah, come on, let's go!' Mark agreed.

They jumped up and started to run down the track towards the car park.

'What's going on?' Allegra asked, suddenly materializing in the air beside them. 'They saw you, Faye!'

Lucy glanced around in alarm but the teenagers had all gone. She became visible as well and Faye did too. Faye was crying.

'What happened to your camouflage?' Lucy demanded.

'I was so shocked when that boy said about the eggs being really valuable I forgot about it and it just disappeared.

What am I going to do? I'm going to be in so much trouble!' Faye wailed.

Lucy put her arm around Faye's shoulders. She was thinking quickly. 'Don't worry. It was only one of the girls who saw you and it was only for a few seconds. She'll think she imagined it when she gets home. No one need know.'

'Yeah,' Allegra agreed. 'At least you camouflaged yourself again really quickly.'

'But I didn't,' Faye replied. 'At least not

straight away. I was too shocked. But then
I disappeared. It was like someone else
camouflaged me.'

'It was me!' The three girls swung
round. Ella was flying towards them. She
looked pale. 'I was watching from the trees
and I saw what happened. I used my
magic to disguise you against the sky until
you got your camouflage back.'

'Oh Ella,' Faye said, flying up to her.
'Thank you!'

Lucy looked at Ella with admiration.
'That was really quick thinking, Ella.' She
realized they all owed Ella an apology.
'Look, I'm sorry we didn't listen to you,'
she said awkwardly. 'We shouldn't have
tried to frighten the teenagers. It was a
stupid thing to do.'

Ella nodded seriously. 'It could have

ended really badly.'

'I know,' Lucy admitted.

'Oh well, no harm done,' Allegra said cheerfully. 'Faye was only seen for a millisecond and we *did* frighten those teenagers away.' She grinned. 'Did you see their faces when they heard me and Lucy making spooky noises? They looked petrified!'

As Lucy remembered the teenagers' expressions she smiled. Allegra was right. It had been very funny!

'I mean, OK, we probably shouldn't have done it,' Allegra carried on blithely, 'but it *was* fun.'

'*Fun!*' Ella looked furious. 'I can't believe you, Allegra! What if more of those teenagers had seen Faye? She would have been in real trouble – we all would and it would have been all your fault.'

Allegra frowned. 'But they didn't see her.'

'But they *could* have done!' Ella exclaimed. 'It was really stupid, Allegra.'

'It wasn't!'

'It was! All your ideas are. You always end up getting us into trouble.'

Allegra looked cross. 'At least I have ideas and I'm not boring like you – boring goody-goody Ella,' she added angrily.

'I'm not a goody-goody!' Ella shouted, tears springing to her eyes. 'And I'm *not* boring! I hate you, Allegra! You haven't even said thank you for saving Faye!' With that she turned and flew away.

'Ella! Wait!' Faye called. But Ella didn't stop. Faye shot a desperate look at Lucy and then flew after her.

Lucy didn't know what to do. Allegra

rarely lost her temper but she was now clearly furious. 'How *dare* Ella say it was all my fault!' she raged. 'It wasn't. I didn't *make* Faye come with us. I didn't *make* her lose her camouflage.'

'No, but . . .' Lucy hesitated. She didn't want to fall out with Allegra but she could see Ella's point. 'Well, Allegra, it *was* our idea and we did persuade Faye to go. I'm not saying it was just your fault,' she added hastily. 'It was mine as well.'

'I notice Ella didn't blame you, did she?' Allegra glared furiously in the direction Ella had gone. 'Everything's always my fault as far as she's concerned! Well, I'm fed up with her!'

Just then Faye came flying back towards them.

'Where's Ella?' Lucy asked.

'She won't come back,' Faye said looking very worried.

'But what about guarding the buzzards?' Lucy asked quickly.

Faye bit her lip. 'She says she's not going to watch with Allegra any more.'

'Suits me just fine,' Allegra declared. 'We can watch the birds for half the night and she can do the rest of the night on her own.'

'I can't let Ella watch on her own!' Faye exclaimed. 'I'll stay with her.'

'If you want,' Allegra said coldly.

'This is silly!' Lucy said, looking from one to the other. 'We should all be watching together. Make Ella come back, Faye.'

Faye looked helpless. 'She won't. She says she's not going to talk to Allegra until Allegra says she's sorry.'

'She'll be waiting a long time then!'
Allegra snapped.

Faye looked over her shoulder. 'I'd better
go. Ella's really upset.' She started to fly
away. 'We'll swap over with you at one.'

'But, Faye . . .' Lucy protested. However,
it was too late. Faye had gone.

Lucy rubbed her forehead. She couldn't
believe what was happening. Allegra and
Ella often bickered but they never had big
fallings-out like this. She looked around
the clearing. It didn't feel right to be there
without the others. 'Maybe you should say
sorry,' she suggested to Allegra.

'No way!' Allegra exclaimed.

Lucy looked at her angry face. She had a
feeling both Allegra and Ella needed some
time to cool down. She sighed. 'I guess we'd
better go and check on the buzzards then.'

★

The honey buzzards were looking restless.
Wendy was sitting on the eggs but she
kept moving and resettling herself. Bob
was perched on a nearby branch, his eyes
darting around.

'I guess all the noise this evening must
have disturbed them,' Lucy said. 'It's OK,'
she said to Wendy, wishing she could make
her understand. 'The people have gone.
There's nothing for you to worry about.'

Wendy didn't look reassured. She
hopped on to the branch and then back
on to the nest, her eyes concerned.

'Let's sit near by and wait,' Lucy said to
Allegra.

The hours passed slowly. Allegra didn't
seem to want to talk much. The birds
finally calmed down and settled to sleep.

Once they were asleep, Allegra didn't suggest any games to play and she didn't chatter like she usually did.

Lucy watched the stars changing in the sky as the night passed. As the autumn star disappeared into the horizon, Faye and Ella came flying to the tree.

'Hi,' Lucy called.

Faye smiled. 'Hello. How have Bob and Wendy been?'

'A bit disturbed,' Lucy replied. 'But they've settled down now.'

'Come on, Lucy,' Allegra said, pointedly ignoring Ella. 'Let's go and see if Xanthe needs us to do anything.'

Lucy hesitated but then gave in. It didn't look like the argument was going to be made up that night. *Maybe tomorrow*, she thought as she and Allegra flew back to the main clearing where all the stardust spirits met each night.

Xanthe was talking to Rebecca near the huge oak tree in the centre of the clearing. She looked surprised to see them.

'What are you doing here?' she asked, hurrying over. 'Is something the matter at the nest?'

'No. Faye and Ella are there,' Allegra replied.

'But you're supposed to be watching together,' Xanthe said. 'It's better if there're four of you, just in case there is any trouble. Then two can go for help and two can watch what's happening.' She frowned. 'You'd better go back.'

Lucy exchanged looks with Allegra. 'We . . . er . . . we've had a bit of an argument

with the others,' she said to Xanthe.

'What about?' Xanthe asked in surprise.

'Oh nothing much,' Lucy lied. If Xanthe found out they had been near humans they would be in major trouble!

'We're not going to guard the birds with them any more,' Allegra said.

Xanthe studied them quizzically. Lucy wondered if she was going to press for more details but, to her relief, Xanthe just shrugged. 'Oh well, if you really feel you can't make it up at the moment then you can get on with another job. Some rare blue ground beetles have been spotted near the oak trees to the east by the river. Can you go over there? It would help us to know how many there are. They're an endangered species so we need to keep an eye on them.'

'Beetles!' Allegra sounded far from
thrilled.

'All animals and insects are equally
worthy of being protected,' Xanthe said,
raising her eyebrows. 'Off you go. Count as
many beetles and as you can find and see
what they're eating. We need to find out
more about their feeding habits.'

Lucy and Allegra flew off.

'I can't believe Xanthe's making us look
at beetles!' Allegra complained. 'We could
have been sent to look at otters or
dormice or badgers or something fun.
Why beetles? They're so dull.'

Blue ground beetles were quite pretty
compared to most beetles – their backs
gleamed an unusual metallic blue colour –
but by the time Lucy had spent an hour
crouching on the ground among damp,

smelly old leaves, turning over rotten logs looking for them, she was in full agreement with Allegra. Watching beetles was the most boring thing she had ever done in the woods.

She thought longingly of the beech tree. It would be so much more fun to be there with Faye and Ella, keeping an eye on the birds and practising their magic. Or they could be playing hide and seek or tag . . .

As Lucy watched a beetle pursuing an unsuspecting slug, she sighed. She really hoped that Allegra and Ella would make up soon!

CHAPTER
Six

Three nights later, Lucy was still waiting
for Allegra and Ella to make friends again.

'I'm *not* making up with her,' Allegra
told Lucy as they sat in the branches of
the buzzards' tree. 'Ella said she hated me.
She has to say sorry first.'

'But you know how stubborn Ella is,'
Lucy protested. 'If you wait for her you
might never make friends and you did say

she was boring and a goody-goody which
. . . well . . . it wasn't very nice.' Her heart
sank at the idea of another night counting
beetles. She was beginning to suspect that
Xanthe was making them do such a
boring task purposefully to make them
sort out the quarrel.

'I suppose it wasn't,' Allegra said
grudgingly. She was silent for a moment.
'My idea *wasn't* stupid, though. We *did*
frighten the teenagers away. They haven't
been back since.' But for the first time, she
sounded slightly unsure that it had been
the right thing to do.

'I know,' Lucy agreed. 'But it could have
ended up really badly.'

Allegra sighed. 'I guess.'

Lucy looked at her hopefully. 'Will you
say sorry then?'

Allegra put up her chin defiantly. 'Not unless Ella says sorry first.'

By the time Faye and Ella came to swap over with them that night, Lucy had made a decision. If Allegra and Ella wouldn't make the first move to apologize then she would have to try to mend their friendship. She'd had more than enough of blue ground beetles!

'Hi, Ella!' she said, flying over.

Ella looked surprised. The last few nights they had all swapped over without speaking. 'Hi,' she said warily.

Lucy took a deep breath. 'Allegra and I were about to practise using our higher powers,' she said. 'We were wondering if you and Faye wanted to do some magic with us? We could all practise together.'

She glanced around and saw Allegra staring at her in surprise. *Please*, Lucy used her eyes to plead silently with Allegra. *Please go along with it.* She saw Allegra hesitate and then to her delight she flew forward.

'Yeah, then we could play tag or something,' she suggested, not quite meeting Ella's eyes.

Lucy felt a wave of relief. It wasn't an apology but she knew it was Allegra's way of trying to make up.

'Oh yes!' Faye said eagerly. 'That would be –'

But before she could finish, Ella interrupted. 'No,' she said coldly. 'We don't want to play tag with you and we don't want to practise our magic with you.' She looked straight at Allegra. 'Not until *you* say sorry.'

A flash of hurt crossed Allegra's eyes but then it was gone and she glared at Ella. 'Well, that's not going to happen! Come on, Lucy!'

She flew off.

Lucy felt like tearing her hair out. Allegra had been prepared to make friends. All Ella had had to do was to say yes to a game of tag, but she couldn't even do that! Shooting an exasperated look at Ella, she flew after Allegra.

'I can't believe how annoying she is!' Allegra fumed as they flew back to the main clearing. 'I mean, I was friendly. Why couldn't she have been friendly back to me?'

'I know,' Lucy agreed as they reached the clearing.

Xanthe saw them land and came over.

'Are you two OK? You look cross.'

'It's Ella!' Allegra exclaimed. 'She's so stubborn! She's driving me mad.'

Xanthe sighed. 'Look, I don't know what this argument you've been having is about but just remember that the things that annoy you about Ella might also be the very things that make her a really good friend.'

'What do you mean?' Allegra demanded.

'Well, Ella might be stubborn, but she's also very brave, determined and loyal. You wouldn't get those good qualities without the stubbornness.'

Allegra sighed. 'I suppose, but it doesn't stop her from being annoying, though!'

Xanthe smiled. 'You and Ella are just very different, Allegra. But that's not bad. It can make you stronger when you work

together. You've each got different
strengths.'

Lucy didn't know what Xanthe meant.
As far as she could see, the differences
between Allegra and Ella only seemed to
make them quarrel.

'Well, I'd better get on,' Xanthe went
on. 'I'll see you both when you've finished
with the beetles. And think about what
I've just said.'

She flew off.

Allegra frowned. 'She just doesn't get
how annoying Ella can be.'

Lucy sighed. 'Come on, I guess we'd
better go and see the beetles.'

By the time Lucy went home that night
she thought that if she saw one more blue
ground beetle she'd scream.

'Stardust be gone!' she whispered as she flew in through her bedroom window and landed softly on the floor.

She felt the familiar heaviness flood through her – like lead running through her veins – and then suddenly she was human again. She looked down. Her golden stardust dress had changed back into her lilac pyjamas.

Yawning, she got into bed. Usually she felt elated after a night as a stardust spirit but tonight she just felt worn out. There was so much stuff running through her head – Allegra, Ella, the argument . . .

Lying back against her pillow she sighed. It really didn't look like they were going to make up.

When Lucy woke at eight thirty the next

morning, she felt ratty and tired. Looking out of the window and seeing the sun shining in a bright blue sky, she pulled on a pair of shorts and a T-shirt and went downstairs.

Hope had gone to stay at a friend's house the night before but Rachel was in the kitchen, eating a slice of toast. She looked up as Lucy came in. 'Hiya.'

'Hi,' Lucy muttered.

'What's up with you?' Rachel asked in surprise.

'Nothing,' Lucy replied. She took some bread out of the bag and put it in the toaster. Sitting down, she sighed.

Rachel leant over and ruffled her hair. 'Cheer up, little sis. It can't be that bad.'

Lucy ducked out from under her hand. 'Stop it!' she said crossly.

'Oooooh,' Rachel said mockingly.
'Going to have a strop, are we?' She raised
her eyebrows. 'You *are* in a mood today.'

'Just leave me alone!' Lucy said.

To her relief just then their mum came
in. 'Morning, love,' Mrs Evans said to Lucy.

'Lucy's in a mood!' Rachel reported.

Lucy glared at her sister.

Mrs Evans looked at her face and
seemed to realize that she wasn't feeling
great. 'Rachel, stop teasing Lucy,' she said,
passing Lucy the toast. 'Is this yours?'

Lucy nodded.

'I'll get some more jam down for you,'
Mrs Evans said, looking at the empty jar
on the table. She dragged a chair over to
the cupboard and stood on it to reach the
top shelf where she kept the jam.

'So what have you got to be upset about

anyway?' Rachel said, glancing at Lucy.

'Lots of things!' Lucy said. 'Important things!'

Rachel raised her eyebrows. 'Now, what could these things be?' She pretended to think. 'Whether to give Thumper carrots or lettuce? Or whether to wear your pink socks or your purple socks.'

Lucy felt her temper snap. 'No! It's things you don't know anything about. Things you wouldn't understand, Rachel!'

'Ooooh,' Rachel said mockingly again.

'Stop it, you two!' Mrs Evans said, turning round in exasperation. 'Why do you always have to –' She broke off with a sudden cry as her feet slipped on the wooden chair.

'Mum!' Lucy and Rachel both cried out in alarm.

'Ow!' Mrs Evans exclaimed as she fell heavily on to the hard tiled floor. She gasped in pain and sat up holding her foot. 'My ankle!'

Seven

Lucy saw her mum go pale and sway slightly. Jumping off her chair she crouched beside her. Putting her arms around her mum's shoulders, she supported her weight.

'Mum!' Rachel said. 'Mum! Are you OK?' Her voice rose in a panic. 'Oh my goodness, what are we going to do?'

'Rachel, shut up!' Lucy snapped. Her

heart was racing but her mind felt strangely in control. She knew they had to stay calm. 'Mum?' she said quietly. 'Are you all right?'

Mrs Evans blinked. 'Oh dear,' she said in a shaky voice. 'I feel a bit peculiar.'

'You should put your head on your knees,' Lucy said, remembering a first-aid class they had done at school. Her teacher had said if someone felt faint it was the best thing to do.

Mrs Evans nodded and Lucy helped support her as she bent over. Her mum drew a sharp intake of breath. 'I've hurt my ankle,' she said through gritted teeth.

'Should we call a doctor – or an ambulance?' Rachel said wildly. 'I'll get the phone. It's 999, isn't it?' She looked almost as pale as Mrs Evans.

'Rachel,' Mrs Evans said weakly, '999 is just for emergencies.'

'But this *is* an emergency!' Rachel exclaimed.

Mrs Evans passed a hand over her eyes.

'Rachel, just call Dad's mobile,' Lucy said. 'But first get me a bag of frozen peas from the freezer.'

'Peas!' Rachel exclaimed, staring at her as if she'd gone mad. 'Mum doesn't want to eat peas!'

'They're for her ankle!' Lucy told her. It was amazing how the things she had learnt in first aid were flooding back into her mind. 'The cold from the peas will keep the swelling down,' she explained.

Rachel ran to the freezer. 'Here.' She virtually threw a bag of peas to Lucy.

'Thanks. Now ring Dad,' Lucy told

her, feeling, for once, as if she was the older sister and not Rachel. She helped their mum into a more comfortable position. 'Should we put these on your foot?' she said, holding out the peas. 'They might help.'

'Good idea,' Mrs Evans said, taking the peas from her. 'And could you get me some cushions or something to put under my leg? If I elevate it that should help keep the swelling down too.'

'Mum, Dad's on the phone!' Rachel said, bringing the receiver over.

Lucy hurried to get some cushions while their mum spoke to their dad. 'I fell off a chair,' Mrs Evans told him. 'No, it's nothing really serious but I think my ankle might be broken.' There was a pause. 'OK, I'll see you soon. Don't worry. Lucy and

Rachel are looking after me. Bye.'

She pressed the off button on the phone. 'Dad's on his way.'

Lucy sighed with relief and saw Rachel do the same.

'Here,' Lucy said, gently putting the cushions under her mum's leg while Mrs Evans held the peas in place. 'Is that comfortable?'

'That's great. Thanks, love,' Mrs Evans replied. She smiled. 'You've been fantastic, Lucy. Thank you.'

Lucy managed a smile back but suddenly, now everything seemed to be under control, she felt rather shaky. She sank down on the floor next to her mum.

'Are you all right?' Mrs Evans asked in concern.

'I'm . . . I'm fine,' Lucy said but she

could feel a lump of tears in her throat. Her mum could have really hurt herself.

'Tell you what. How about I get us all a drink?' Rachel said. 'Tea for you, Mum? Coke, Lucy?'

'Thanks, love,' Mrs Evans replied. 'I think we could all do with something.'

Rachel fetched two cans of Coke and then put the kettle on to make a cup of tea. 'Here,' she said, handing a can to Lucy.

As Lucy sipped the cold sweet Coke she began to feel slightly better.

Rachel carefully carried a cup of tea over for their mum. She looked much calmer now. She sat down beside Mrs Evans. 'Are you OK, Mum?'

Mrs Evans nodded. 'It just hurts quite a lot.'

'Shall I tell you a joke?' Rachel asked. 'It might stop you thinking about it.'

'All right,' Mrs Evans agreed.

'What did the man with the broken leg say to the nurse?'

Mrs Evans smiled weakly. 'I don't know, what did he say?'

Rachel's eyes twinkled. 'I've got a crutch on you!'

'Oh Rachel,' Mrs Evans said, shaking her head as she and Lucy both grinned.

By the time Mr Evans got home, Rachel had told thirteen more doctor jokes. Mr Evans came into the kitchen looking very worried but his face relaxed when he saw them all laughing. 'So what's been happening?' he asked.

Mrs Evans explained. 'Rachel and Lucy have been fantastic,' she said.

'Actually it was Lucy who was fantastic,' Rachel said, looking rather shamefaced. 'I was useless. It was Lucy who organized everything and helped Mum.' She glanced at Lucy, her face serious for once. 'You were great, Luce.'

Lucy could hardly believe her ears. Rachel never said anything nice to her. 'It wasn't just me. You helped too,' she said awkwardly.

'No, I didn't,' Rachel said.

Mrs Evans squeezed her hand. 'You did, Rachel. I know Lucy was the most help when the accident happened but the jokes you've been telling almost made me forget about my ankle hurting.' She glanced from Rachel to Lucy. 'You both helped me – just in different ways.'

A memory flickered across Lucy's mind. It was something Xanthe had said the night before about how different people had different strengths and how differences

could make people stronger when they
worked together. But she didn't have time
to think about it right then. Her dad was
helping her mum up. 'I'm going to take
Mum to hospital,' he said. 'Will you two
be OK here?'

Rachel and Lucy nodded and helped
their mum to the car.

When the car had disappeared out of
sight, they turned and went back indoors.

'What are you going to do now?'
Rachel asked.

'I think I'll go up to my bedroom,' Lucy
answered. She wanted some time to think.

'All right, see you later,' Rachel said,
sitting down on the sofa. As she sat down
she looked over her shoulder. 'Lucy?'

'Yeah,' Lucy replied, stopping on the stairs.

Rachel hesitated. 'I . . . I'm glad you

were here today.'

'I'm glad you were too,' Lucy said.

They smiled at each other and then Lucy carried on up the stairs feeling suddenly light-footed. It was so nice not to be arguing with Rachel for once; to actually feel really pleased that her sister was there.

Sitting down on her bed, she thought

back over what Xanthe had said. Maybe differences *were* good. After all, she and Rachel had helped their mum in different ways.

I guess it's the same with me, Allegra, Ella and Faye, Lucy thought. *We're all good at different things and it's because we're all different from each other. Allegra's daring, Ella's sensible, Faye's thoughtful and as for me . . .*

Well, she wasn't sure what she was like but she was certainly different from the others.

Suddenly Allegra and Ella's argument seemed even dumber than ever. She went to the phone and punched in Faye's number.

'Hello,' Faye answered.

'Hi, it's me – Lucy.'

'Hi, Lucy,' Faye said in surprise.

Lucy came straight to the point. 'Look, we

have to get Allegra and Ella to make friends.'

'I know,' Faye agreed. 'But what can we do? Ella's not just being stubborn, Lucy. She's really hurt that Allegra called her boring and didn't even thank her for helping when my camouflage disappeared.'

Lucy sighed. 'Poor Ella. But Allegra's feeling really hurt too, and, after all, her idea of scaring the teenagers did work.'

'It's awful. This argument's making them both so unhappy,' Faye said.

'Yes,' Lucy agreed. 'And it's making you and me miserable too. Tonight let's refuse to leave the clearing until they're friends again. We've just got to get them to make up.'

'I suppose we can try,' Faye said, not sounding very hopeful.

'We'll do more than try,' Lucy declared decisively. 'We'll *make* it happen!'

Eight

Later that night, Ella and Faye flew into the clearing to swap places with Lucy and Allegra.

'Come on, let's go,' Allegra said abruptly.

'No.' Lucy looked squarely at Allegra. She hadn't warned her about her plans because she hadn't wanted to give Allegra a chance to argue. 'I'm not leaving this clearing until you and Ella make up.' She flew over to Ella. 'Faye and I both think this argument's stupid, Ella. It's making you and Allegra miserable. Can't you just forgive each other so we can start going round together again?'

Ella swung round to look at Faye. 'Have you been talking to Lucy?'

Faye went red but nodded and flew over to Lucy's side. 'Please can't you two just make up?' she pleaded.

'I'll make up when Allegra says she's sorry,' Ella said coldly.

'Why should I?' Allegra replied angrily.

'Because otherwise this will go on forever!' Lucy told her. 'You're both to blame and –'

She broke off as she heard an unusual noise. It was the drone of a motorbike's engine. She looked around. From the startled expressions on her friends' faces it was obvious they had heard it too.

'That's a motorbike!' Allegra exclaimed.

'What's someone doing riding a motorbike round here at this time of night?' Ella said.

'I don't know,' Lucy said, feeling worried.

The motorbike seemed to be heading straight towards them through the trees. It got closer and closer and then suddenly it stopped and the engine was turned off.

'What's going on?' Faye whispered. 'It sounds like it's in the clearing over there.'

'Maybe it's someone after the buzzards' eggs,' Ella hissed.

They heard a boy's voice. 'Come on, Dave. It's this way.'

Lucy recognized the voice. 'It's one of those boys from the other night!' she gasped.

There was a cracking of twigs under feet.

'Quick!' Allegra whispered in alarm. 'Camouflage yourselves!'

In an instant the girls had all disappeared.

Two boys came through the trees. Lucy recognized them as the two that had been talking the other night about buzzards' eggs being valuable. Dave and Mark, she thought they were called. They were wearing black leather motorcycling clothes and the shorter one, Mark, was carrying a stick.

Dave looked around. 'This place is well creepy.'

'Let's just get the eggs and get out,' Mark said grimly.

Get the eggs! Lucy stared in horror.

'What are we going to do?' Faye's panicked whisper came out of the air.

'One of us should go and get help,' Ella suggested.

'There isn't time,' said Lucy frantically as the boys hurried towards the tree.

'They're going to get the eggs!' Faye whispered, almost in tears.

Think! Lucy told herself. But it was too late. Mark was swinging himself up to the nest.

Wendy called out in alarm and flew into the air. As Mark hauled himself on to the branch she lashed out at him with her taloned feet. Bob shrieked loudly and flew at the boy, snapping his beak at him.

'Get away!' Mark growled. He swung the stick menacingly. Both birds flew upwards, squawking wildly.

Lucy felt utterly helpless. It was all happening so fast. If only they could get help. But there was no time. Mark reached into the nest and pulled out one of the eggs. It gleamed in the starlight. 'Here, Dave, take this,' Mark said, passing it down to his friend. 'I'll get the other.' As Dave climbed down, Mark waved his stick at Bob again. 'Get away with you!'

But as he did so he failed to notice Wendy swooping down from behind him.

Her talons raked at his head, pulling out a
clump of hair.

Giving a cry of alarm, Mark swished
wildly with his stick. It hit Wendy's
outstretched wing.

With a squawk of pain, she spiralled
downwards.

'Mark! You've hurt her!' Dave gasped.
'You said we wouldn't hurt them. You said
we'd just take the eggs.'

'I . . . I couldn't help it. She was
attacking me!' Mark stammered.

Bob swooped down in fury, his claws
and beak aimed at the teenager's face.
Mark retreated, half falling down the tree
in his haste to escape. 'Quick! Let's go!' he
yelled to Dave.

They began to run through the trees
with Dave holding the egg in his hand.

'We've got to do something!' Lucy gasped, materializing. She looked around and saw the others. The shock had made them all lose their camouflage. Faye was crying.

'Come on! We can stop them before they get on their motorbike,' Allegra said.

'No!' Ella exclaimed. 'We shouldn't go. At least not —'

'Ella!' Allegra shouted furiously. 'How can you say we shouldn't go? This is an emergency! Don't you *care* about the eggs?'

'Of course I do!' Ella exclaimed. 'I'm just trying to say —'

'Forget it!' Allegra interrupted. 'You can be sensible if you want. I'm going to save that egg!'

Plunging into the sky she flew after the boys. Seeing the hurt look on Ella's face,

Lucy hesitated but Allegra was right. They *had* to save the eggs! She raced after Allegra. Out of the corner of her eye she saw Faye shoot an apologetic glance at Ella and join them too.

The three of them raced through the trees. They could see the boys just ahead of them on the path. They had almost reached the clearing where their motorbike was parked.

'I've had an idea!' Allegra streaked ahead, disappearing in mid air.

'What's she doing?' Faye asked Lucy.

'I don't know,' Lucy answered. Knowing Allegra it could be anything!

There was a sudden crack and then just ahead of the boys a large branch fell from a tree across the track.

'Allegra!' Lucy exclaimed. 'I bet that

was her!'

Mark and Dave cried out in alarm. They tried to stop but they were too close to the branch and they tripped over.

'The egg!' Lucy gasped as the buzzards' egg flew out of Dave's hand. 'It's going to break!' She stared in horror as the egg catapulted upwards. They might have stopped the boys but they hadn't saved the egg unless . . . An idea came to her.

'*Shield*,' she whispered desperately, shutting her eyes and picturing Leo with all her might, '*be with me!*'

Magic seemed to flow into her from the stars. Opening her eyes she pointed at the egg. It plummeted downwards and bounced as it hit the ground. Lucy saw it disappear unharmed over the edge of the bank the track was on.

'*Shield be with me! Shield be with me!*' she whispered over and over again, hoping the egg had landed safely. She didn't dare go and look because the boys were standing right by the bank's edge.

'The egg, Dave! You dropped it!' Mark shouted. 'You idiot!'

'That . . . that branch just seemed to fall out of thin air!' Dave stammered, staring at the branch.

Mark looked over the bank. 'The egg must have broken. I can't see it.'

Just then Lucy saw Allegra fly up beside her. She was still partly camouflaged, her body a faint outline against the starry sky. 'Lucy?'

Lucy let her camouflage fade a little. 'I'm here!' she whispered.

'Me too,' Faye said quietly.

'You made that branch fall, didn't you?'
Lucy said to Allegra.

'Yes but I hadn't thought Dave might
drop the egg,' Allegra hissed. 'I saw it bounce
– was that you putting a shield around it?'

Lucy nodded.

'Oh Lucy!' Allegra said in relief. 'That
was a brilliant idea.'

'I don't know if it's worked, though,'
Lucy said.

'The boys are moving away,' Allegra
whispered, nodding towards where Dave
and Mark were moving down the track.
They seemed to be arguing. 'Let's go and
see if we can find the egg.'

Lucy and Faye nodded and they flew
silently to the bank. There was thick
undergrowth running down the slope.
Hovering above it the girls scanned the

brambles. Suddenly Lucy saw a glimpse
of white.

'There!' she gasped.

The egg was nestled deep in the roots of
a bramble bush. Lucy flew down and
pulled it out. The thorns tore at her hands
but she didn't care. 'It's OK!' she
exclaimed.

'Oh Lucy, well done!' Faye said,
hugging her.

Lucy felt a rush of relief tinged with pride. She'd done it! Her magic had saved the egg.

'Come on, let's take it back to the nest before it gets cold,' Allegra said.

'We'd better be quiet, though,' Faye warned. 'The boys are still there.'

Lucy tucked the egg safely into the pocket in her dress and they flew upwards. The boys were still on the track. Lucy held her breath and tried to fly around them as silently as possible. But as she did so she heard Mark say something that made her blood turn to ice.

'Let's just go back and get the other egg.'

'I think we should just forget the whole thing,' Dave said, looking around anxiously. 'I don't like this place.' He ducked suddenly. 'What was that? I felt something fly near my head. I'm sure I did. Maybe it was a bat!' His voice rose in alarm.

'Stop messing around,' Mark told him. 'We've got to go back and get the other egg. Think of the money.'

'But . . .'

'Come on!' Mark insisted. He picked up his stick from where it had fallen when he tripped over and started to march back along the track. Dave hesitated and then hurried after him, looking around anxiously.

'They're going back!' Lucy exclaimed in alarm. 'They're going to steal the other egg!'

Nine

Lucy, Allegra and Faye flew towards the clearing as fast as they could. They quickly overtook the boys.

'What are we going to do?' Faye gasped.

Lucy's mind was running through possibilities. 'Can you conjure some rain, Faye? That might stop them.'

'They're not going to mind getting wet,' Allegra said. 'Fire would be better.'

'But it might scare the birds and make them abandon the nest,' Lucy said as they swooped into the clearing.

They all stopped in mid air and stared.

'Where *is* the nest?' Faye said in astonishment.

Lucy blinked. The nest had gone! Where the large straggly pile of twigs and branches had been there was just an empty branch covered in green leaves. Her mind reeled in confusion. What was happening? 'We . . . we are in the right clearing, aren't we?' she stammered. Even as the words left her mouth she knew it was a stupid question. Of *course* they were in the right clearing. After spending every night here for the last five nights, she knew it well enough.

Just then the boys came hurrying into the clearing and the girls flew high into the trees. Mark was talking. 'I'll keep the birds away. You get the egg then we get out of here. OK?'

Dave stared at the beech tree.

'OK?' Mark repeated.

'Uh, Mark?' Dave pointed. 'Where's the nest?'

Mark looked at the empty branch and his mouth dropped open. 'It's not there!' He looked around. 'We must have come to the wrong clearing.'

'We can't have done,' Dave replied.

'Well, nests don't just disappear, do they?' Mark said.

Lucy's eyes widened. Of course! Why hadn't she thought about it before? 'It's Ella!' she hissed to the others. 'I bet she's disguising the nest!'

Faye and Allegra stared at her.

'Yeah!' Faye said. 'That's why we can't see it.'

'Of course,' Allegra said. 'It's there. It just looks different.'

'Or at least it will for as long as the spell holds out,' Lucy said.

'We have to get rid of the boys before Ella loses concentration,' Faye said quickly.

Lucy glanced down at the boys. Mark was still staring around the clearing in confusion. How were they going to get rid of him and Dave?

Dave was looking worried. 'Come on, let's go. This place is seriously freaking me out. Branches dropping, nests disappearing.' He ducked again suddenly, waving his arms as if trying to knock something away. 'What *was* that? I felt something flying round my head again!'

He looked around.

'You know, I think Dave's scared of bats!' Allegra whispered suddenly. 'Let me see!'

She shut her eyes and her lips moved. For a moment, a look of intense concentration crossed her face.

'Yes!' she hissed, opening her eyes. 'I've just seen it in his heart. He's really terrified of bats. He's worried they're going to fly at him and get caught in his hair.' She looked at Faye and Lucy. 'This is brilliant!'

'It is?' said Faye, looking mystified. 'Why?'

'Because we can use it to scare him and Mark away. If we camouflage ourselves we can fly around their heads, grabbing at their hair. They'll think we're bats and run away. Even though Mark's not really scared of bats I bet there's no way he'll stay here on his own.'

'They came on the same motorbike,' Faye put in. 'So if Dave goes, Mark will have to.'

There was no time to waste. Lucy made an instant decision. 'Come on. Let's do it!'

In a second they had camouflaged themselves.

'Good luck!' Allegra whispered. 'And don't let yourself be seen!'

Lucy felt the air move and then Allegra was gone. A moment later, Dave ducked and reached for his head. 'What was that?' he said, looking around. 'I definitely felt something! Mark! Mark! There's something flying around me!' He ducked again. 'There it is again!' he exclaimed, swiping through the air. 'It's a bat. I *know* it's a bat!'

'Don't be daft!' Mark said.

Lucy was sure she heard a stifled giggle from Allegra.

Grinning to herself, she dived down through the sky. She could see Mark's thick brown hair. She reached out and tugged a handful. He jumped about a metre in the air.

'What the . . .!' he shouted.

Lucy swooped away and then dived in again.

'Arghhh!' Mark cried, dropping the stick.

Lucy poked his ear.

'What's going on?' Mark said in panic. 'What's happening?'

The two boys swung their hands wildly around their heads.

'It's bats!' Dave yelled, his face pale. 'They're attacking us!'

'Arghhh!' both boys shouted as Lucy,

Allegra and Faye grabbed at them at the
same time.

'Let's get out of here, Dave!' Mark
exclaimed.

'*Run!*' Dave yelled.

They charged blindly through the trees,
tripping and stumbling.

Within seconds they were out of sight.

Lucy, Faye and Allegra uncamouflaged
themselves. Allegra was laughing so hard
that tears were running down her face.

'Did you see how scared they were?'

Lucy gasped between giggles.

'They were terrified!' Faye cried.

Allegra flung her hands in the air, mimicking Dave. 'Bats! Bats! They're attacking me!'

The three of them burst out laughing again.

'That was brilliant! Well done!' Lucy, Allegra and Faye swung round. Ella was hovering in the air behind them.

'Ella!' Faye squealed, flying over and hugging her in relief.

'Is the egg safe?' Ella asked quickly.

'Yes,' Lucy said, pulling it out of her pocket. 'I've got it here.' She swooped over. 'You disguised the nest with your magic, Ella, didn't you?'

Ella nodded. 'I thought the boys might come back.' She glanced reproachfully at

Allegra. 'That's what I was trying to say
when you flew after them. I wasn't saying
we shouldn't go, just that maybe *some* of us
should stay here and look after the
remaining egg.'

'Oh,' Allegra said, looking taken aback.

Lucy could see the hurt in Ella's eyes.

'I *do* care about the birds. I really do,'
Ella said quietly.

Allegra hesitated and then suddenly she
flew forward. 'Oh Ella, I'm sorry!' she
exclaimed, hugging her. 'I shouldn't have said
you didn't care about the birds. If you hadn't
stayed here and done your magic then the
boys would have got the egg. You were
fantastic! Can we be friends again? I'm really
sorry we argued and I called you boring. I
didn't mean it. You aren't boring, you're just
sensible – much more sensible than me. If it

hadn't been for you Faye would have been seen by all the teenagers instead of just one and the egg would have been stolen.'

'Maybe, but you got the first egg back and you frightened the boys away,' Ella told her. 'It was a brilliant idea to read that boy's heart.'

'I guess we all used our magic,' Allegra said. 'We all helped.'

'I didn't,' Faye put in quietly. 'You and Lucy and Ella all used your magic but I didn't do anything. I've not been much use.'

'But you can be now,' Ella said. 'Do you think you can do some healing magic? Wendy is hurt. I put her over there behind a bush to keep her safe from the boys but she needs help. I made her as comfortable as possible but I think her wing might be broken. Come and see.'

'We should put the egg back first,'
Lucy said.

The others nodded and they flew to
the nest.

Bob looked at them anxiously. As Lucy
slipped the egg back into the nest he
chattered his beak at her and flapped his
wings unhappily.

'He's been really upset,' Ella said. 'He's
been pacing around on the branch and
keeps flying down to Wendy and then
flying back here.'

'So where is Wendy?' Allegra asked.

'This way.' Ella led the way over to a
hazel bush tucked at the side of the
clearing. 'Here.'

Wendy was lying on the ground. One of
her wings was hanging at a strange angle
and her bright eyes looked dull with pain.

Lucy bit her lip. Wendy looked in a bad way. 'Do you think you'll be able to help her?' she asked Faye anxiously.

Faye swallowed. 'I'll try.'

CHAPTER

Ten

Faye walked up to the bird. Wendy drew
her head back in alarm. 'Hush, it's OK,'
Faye whispered, kneeling down beside her.

Wendy watched her warily.

'Do you think you'll be able to heal
her?' Allegra asked softly.

'I don't know,' Faye replied. 'I've never
healed a broken bone before.' She reached
out her hand towards Wendy's injured wing.

'Be careful,' Ella gasped, as Wendy snapped her curved beak.

Faye moved slowly. 'It's OK,' she murmured, her eyes fixed on the bird's. She laid her hand very gently against Wendy's wing. 'I'm going to make you better.' She shut her eyes. '*Healing be with me!*'

Lucy held her breath.

There was a long moment of silence.

'Look,' Ella breathed, pointing at the bird.

Lucy stared. The pain was slowly leaving Wendy's eyes. The bird lifted her head as if in amazement and looked at her wing.

Faye opened her eyes and lifted her hand.

Wendy flapped her wing. It moved properly up and down.

'Faye, you've done it!' Lucy whispered as Faye sat back. 'You've made her better!'

Wendy lifted her head and stretched out

both beautiful wings. The browny-grey
feathers rippled and shone in the starlight.
She stepped forward, flapped her wings
and the next minute she had taken off.
Tucking her feet under her she flew
upwards into the sky.

The four girls watched as the majestic
bird soared through the night sky, her
great wings beating as she flew towards the
beech tree.

There was a delighted caw and then
Bob flew to meet her. The two birds
circled around each other and then headed
back to the nest. As they landed they
touched beaks gently.

Lucy felt as if a heavy weight had just
fallen from her shoulders. Turning to the
others she saw the relief on their faces.
'We did it!' she said. 'We protected them –

and their eggs.'

'Only just,' Allegra said.

'Wasn't it lucky we were all here?' Faye said. 'If it had just been two of us, we'd never have been able to stop those boys.'

Lucy shivered. It was a horrible thought but Faye was right. Two of them on their own, like her and Allegra, wouldn't have stood a chance of stopping Dave and Mark. From the looks on the others' faces it was clear they were thinking the same thing.

'We mustn't *ever* argue again,' Ella said.

'We're so much stronger when we work together,' Faye said.

'Xanthe told me and Allegra that yesterday,' Lucy told them. 'She said that the differences between us are good and that we shouldn't argue about them. She was right. Ella, you managed to save the

second egg because you were sensible and
realized someone needed to stay here, but
then we wouldn't have got the first egg
back if it hadn't been for Allegra racing
after the boys.'

Ella nodded. 'Yeah, I guess we are all good at different things. I'm sensible. Allegra has great ideas. Faye's brilliant at noticing when someone's upset or unhappy and you're really brave, Lucy, *and* you organize us all and get things done. I guess we really do work best as a team.'

'So let's *always* be a team,' Lucy declared. 'Agreed?' She looked at her friends.

'Agreed!' they all said, hugging.

As they broke apart, Lucy glanced up at the buzzards' nest. Wendy was flapping her wings and Bob was pacing up and down the branch. They looked restless.

'I hope the birds settle down again soon,' she said. 'They seem a bit agitated.'

'Yeah,' Ella agreed, looking up. 'They must have been really upset by everything that's been going on tonight.'

A frown creased Allegra's forehead. 'You don't think they'll leave the nest, do you? I know that sometimes if nesting birds are disturbed too much they abandon their eggs.'

Worry ran through Lucy. After everything that had happened she couldn't bear the thought that the birds might decide to abandon their eggs. 'I wish there was a way we could let them know that they are safe now, that the boys have gone and won't be coming back.'

'I know,' Ella agreed. 'But there's nothing we can do.'

Just then another stardust spirit came flying into the clearing. 'Xanthe!' Faye exclaimed.

'Is everything all right here?' Xanthe

asked as she landed beside them. 'I saw a motorbike leaving the woods at high speed. It seemed to be coming from this direction so I thought I'd better come and check that you and the birds were all OK.'

'We are now,' Allegra told her. 'At least I hope the birds are,' she added, glancing anxiously at the nest.

'What's been happening?' Xanthe questioned.

The girls quickly told her.

'So you managed to save the eggs by all using your magic?' Xanthe exclaimed. 'Well done! Of course,' she added hastily, 'you shouldn't have used magic around the boys. You're not experienced enough yet, but,' she smiled in relief, 'I'm glad you did.'

'We're just worried about the birds now,' Lucy said, relieved that they weren't going to get into trouble. 'They seem really upset.'

'Do you think they might abandon the nest?' Allegra asked her mum. 'They might think the boys will come back.'

Xanthe looked at the birds. 'It's OK, I can do something,' she said. 'You can come and watch if you want.'

She flew into the air.

Lucy and the others exchanged mystified looks and then quickly flew after Xanthe as she headed towards the nest.

The birds looked at her suspiciously. Wendy flapped off the nest and perched on the branch beside Bob. Xanthe stopped about a metre away and murmured soothingly to them. They watched her warily.

Xanthe flew closer and gently touched a hand on each of their heads. Lucy saw both birds stiffen. Xanthe's lips began to move.

It was impossible to hear what she was saying but, whatever it was, the birds seemed to understand. As Xanthe spoke, the tension seemed to melt away from them. Their bodies relaxed and their eyes lost their agitated expression.

Wendy let out a soft caw and then, tilting her head, she rubbed her cheek against Xanthe's hand.

Bob fluttered his wings and nodded his head.

Xanthe moved back. 'Stay and be happy,' she said softly. 'They'll be OK now,' she said, flying back to the girls.

'What did you do?' Allegra demanded.

'It was like you were talking to them,' Lucy said.

'I was,' Xanthe replied.

The four girls stared at her.

'They could *understand* you?' Ella
questioned.

Xanthe nodded. 'I told them that the
boys had gone and that they would not be
disturbed again. I said we would grow a
grove of brambles around their tree and
this area to protect them.'

'But how could you talk to them? I
didn't think anyone could talk to animals,'
Faye questioned.

'It's a type of stardust magic,' Xanthe
replied.

'Can we learn it?' Lucy asked. Talking to
animals sounded amazing!

'Maybe one day,' Xanthe said. 'But it
takes a lot of power to communicate
directly with animals and only a very few
stardust spirits can do it. You've got a lot to

learn before you can use that sort of magic. Still,' she smiled at them, 'you're not doing too badly. You've worked really well as a team today and you've learnt the most important stardust lesson of all – that working with others makes you stronger.' Her eyes scanned their faces and her voice became suddenly serious. 'Trouble comes when stardust spirits work on their own. When that happens it is easy to get too caught up in the love of power, but that way darkness lies.' For a moment, Xanthe's eyes seemed to linger on Lucy and Lucy had the strangest feeling that she was talking directly to her. But then Xanthe's gaze moved on. 'I hope none of you ever forget what you've learnt today,' she told them all.

They were shaking their heads when a

faint tapping sound carried through the air towards them.

'What's that noise?' Allegra asked, frowning.

Xanthe looked puzzled. 'It sounds like –' She broke off. 'Of course! It's the eggs. The buzzard chicks are hatching out!'

The serious mood immediately disappeared.

'The chicks!' Allegra exclaimed. 'Can we see?'

Xanthe nodded and they all flew up to the nest.

The eggs had cracks running down their sides and as the girls watched a beak appeared through the shell of one. The chick inside started pecking a hole.

Lucy watched spellbound as the hole got bigger and finally the egg cracked apart. A

small, bedraggled white chick sat in the
nest and looked around with bright, dark,
astonished eyes.

'*Cheep!*' it blurted out.

It looked so comical that the girls started
to laugh.

'Isn't it cute!' Lucy exclaimed.

'The other one's hatching too!' Allegra
said, grabbing her arm. 'Look!'

Soon two chicks were sitting in the nest.
Their damp coats were drying and
becoming fluffy and white. Perching on
the edge of the nest, Wendy gently stroked
their heads with her curved beak. Bob
watched protectively from the branch.

'I can't believe they've hatched out
safely,' Faye said in delight. 'Isn't it
wonderful?'

'Wonderful!' Xanthe echoed, putting an

arm around Lucy's and Allegra's shoulders. 'And it's all thanks to you four girls. You saved them.'

'Together,' Lucy said, looking at her friends.

They grinned at each other. 'Together,' they chorused.

Do you love magic, unicorns and fairies?

Join the sparkling

Linda Chapman

fan club today!

It's FREE!

You will receive a sparkle pack, including:

Stickers   **Badge**
Membership card   **Glittery pencil**

Plus four Linda Chapman newsletters every year,
packed full of fun, games, news and competitions.
And look out for a special card on your birthday!

How to join:

Visit lindachapman.co.uk and enter your details

Send your name, address, date of birth* and email address (if you have one) to:
**Linda Chapman Fan Club, Puffin Marketing,
80 Strand, London, WC2R 0RL**

Your details will be kept by Puffin only for the purpose of sending information regarding Linda Chapman
and other relevant Puffin books. It will not be passed on to any third parties.
You will receive your free introductory pack within 28 days

*If you are under 13, you must get permission from a parent or guardian

Notice to parent/guardian of children under 13 years old: Please add the following to their email/letter including
your name and signature: I consent to my child/ward submitting his/her personal details as above.